THIS BOOK BELONGS TO

_____

PUPS SAVE A BASKETBALL GAME

Let's **play ball!**

On a beautiful day in Adventure Bay, Skye, Rocky and Marshall were playing basketball while Mayor Goodway watched from the sidelines.

"Here comes the famous Dalmatian Dunk!" said Marshall, leaping into the sky.

But instead of making the shot, Marshall flew across the court on top of the ball and crash landed in Mayor Humdingers lap!

"Hmmmmf!" grunted Mayor Humdinger. "If your pups need some lessons, my undefeated Foggy Bottom Boomers basketball team would be happy to help."

"Ha! If your basketball team played our basketball team, they wouldn't be undefeated for long!" said Mayor Goodway.

The two mayors both thought their team was the best! So they agreed to have a basketball game. But Mayor Goodway forgot one thing: Adventure Bay didn't have a basketball team!

"Oh, no!" said Mayor Goodway. "What are we going to do?"

"Whenever there's an emergency, we call Ryder," said Rocky.

On the PupPad, Ryder listened as Mayor Goodway explained the problem. But Ryder wasn't worried.

"No job is too big, no pup is too small...for basketball!" With that, he called the pups to the Lookout!

All the pups lined up in front of Ryder.

Mayor Goodway arrived as Ryder explained they only had one day to assemble a basketball team and defeat the Foggy Bottom Boomers!

Ryder asked Chase to use his whistle, megaphone and traffic cones to set up a basketball practice. Then he asked Marshall to stand by with his EMT gear, water and ice, to make sure that no one overheated.

They were Adventure Bay's new basketball team! They rushed off to their first practice.

At the basketball court, Chase was doing an awesome job training the rest of the pups. Mayor Goodway and Chickaletta cheered them on from the sidelines.

"It's going to be a great game!" shouted the mayor.

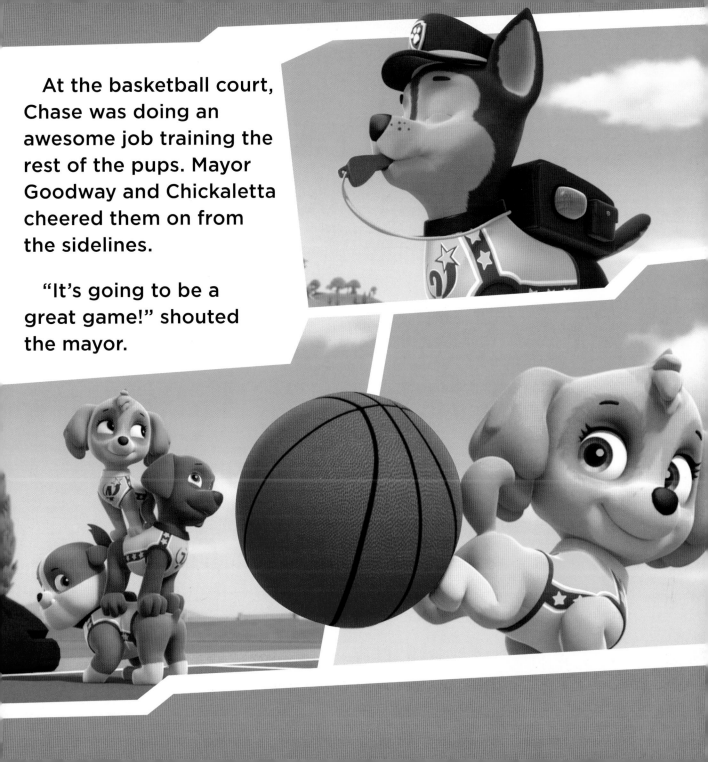

The next day, the pups arrived at the basketball court in their new Adventure Bay All-Star uniforms. The Foggy Bottom Boomers were there already, shooting hoop after hoop!

"Is that who we're playing?" asked Marshall, as the pups gulped in unison.

But Ryder was hopeful that the pups stood a chance. "Let's shoot some hoops!" he said.

All of the pups but Marshall hurried onto the court.

"If someone gets hurt, I want to be ready, Ryder," said Marshall. "Are you sure that's the reason?" Ryder asked.

Ryder said Marshall didn't have to play. "But if you change your mind, let us know."

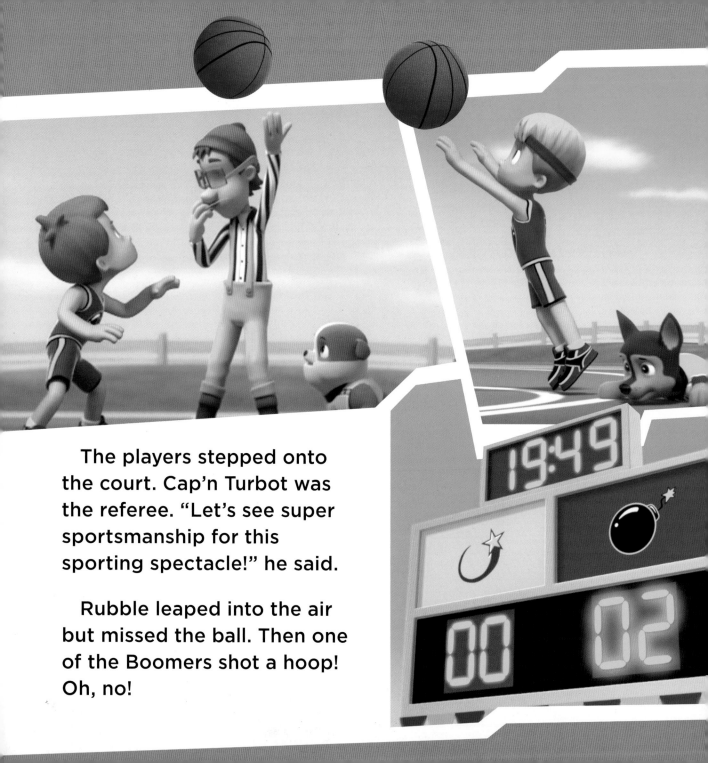

The players stepped onto the court. Cap'n Turbot was the referee. "Let's see super sportsmanship for this sporting spectacle!" he said.

Rubble leaped into the air but missed the ball. Then one of the Boomers shot a hoop! Oh, no!

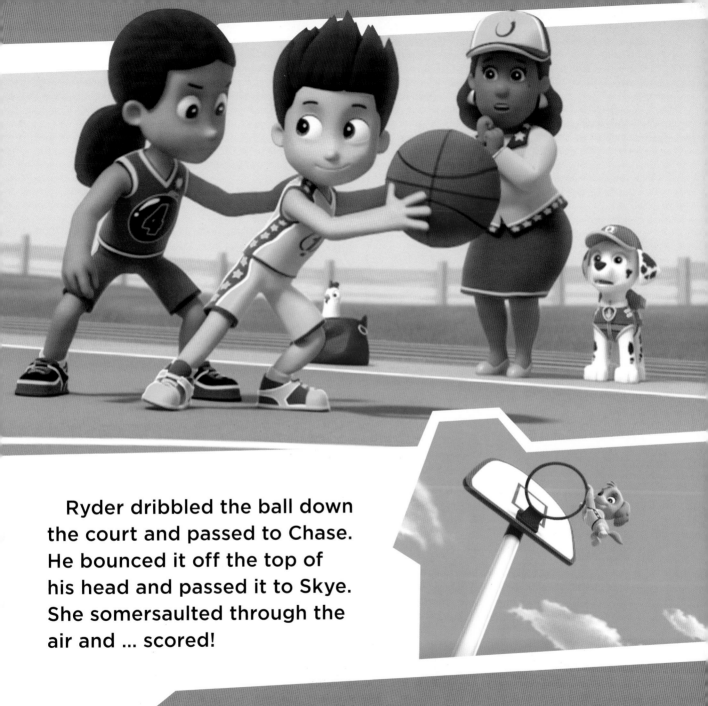

Ryder dribbled the ball down the court and passed to Chase. He bounced it off the top of his head and passed it to Skye. She somersaulted through the air and ... scored!

"Alriiight!"

"Go Allstars!" cheered Mayor Goodway.

Chickaletta joined in, flapping her wings as the pups worked together as a team and continued to score.

At half-time, the pups were ahead!

Mayor Humdinger twirled his moustache, annoyed. He called over one of his players and whispered, "You know what to do ..."

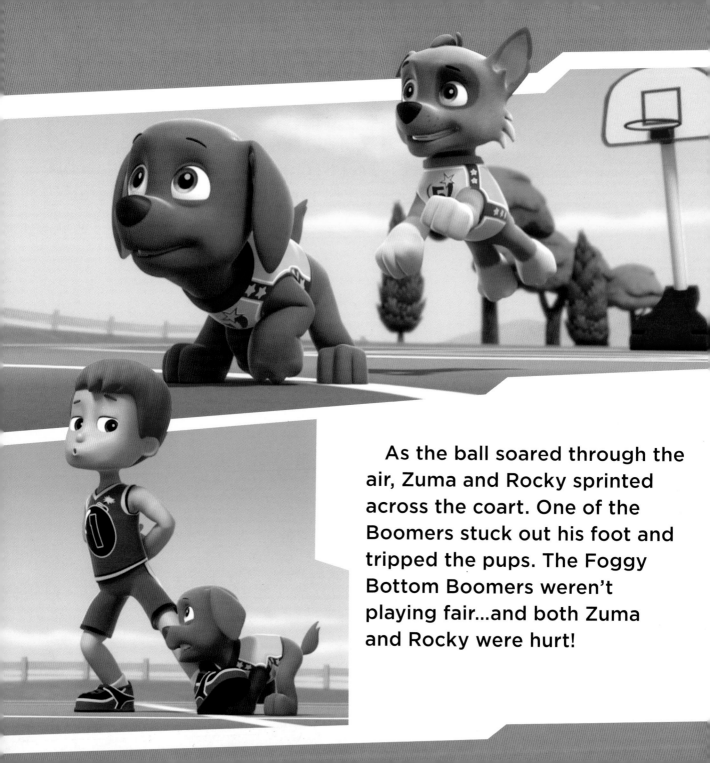

As the ball soared through the air, Zuma and Rocky sprinted across the coart. One of the Boomers stuck out his foot and tripped the pups. The Foggy Bottom Boomers weren't playing fair...and both Zuma and Rocky were hurt!

Cap'n Turbot blew his whistle and called, "Foul on the unfriendly Foggy Bottoms for forcing that flippity- flop!"

Ryder ran over to the pups. "Oh, no! Marshall, Zuma and Rocky need emergency medical attention!"

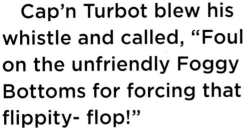

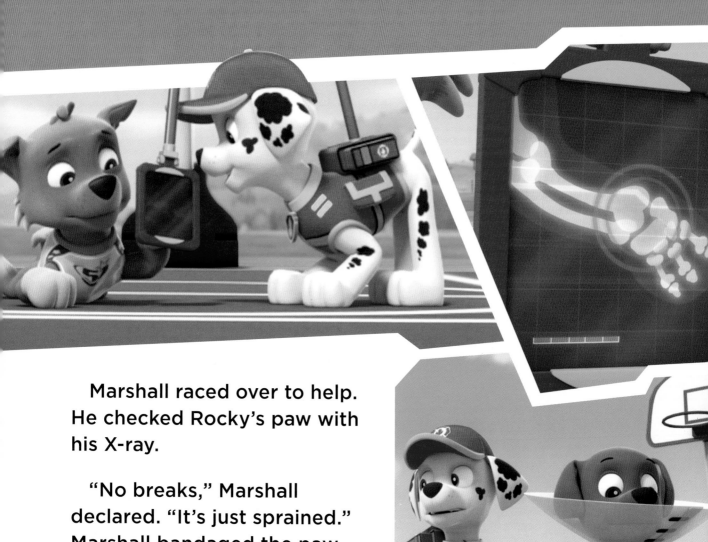

Marshall raced over to help. He checked Rocky's paw with his X-ray.

"No breaks," Marshall declared. "It's just sprained." Marshall bandaged the paw. Then he put ice on Zuma's tail to stop it from swelling.

But now the team was missing two players!

Ryder asked Marshall if he wanted to play.

"Ryder," said Marshall. "I'm kinda clumsy with the ball."

"It doesn't matter how good you are," said Chase. "You're a part of the team. No game is too big, no pup is too small!"

"Ok, I'll try!" replied Marshall.

The All-Stars trotted onto the court. When Ryder missed a foul shot, Marshall dove for the rebound, but a Boomer beat him to it.

Ryder consoled the fire pup. "You'll get it next time, Marshall."

It was the final seconds of the game. Both mayors were super nervous. The Adventure Bay All-Stars and the Foggy Bottom Boomers were neck and neck!

Ahhhhh!

Ryder passed the ball to Marshall. The dalmatian landed on top of the ball.

"Whoaaaaa!" Marshall said as he rolled right past the Boomers' defense, bounced into the air...and into the basket!

Mayor Goodwayy and the pups jumped for joy!

"You won the game," said Skye.

Marshall managed to squeeze himself through the hoop and landed in Ryder's hands.

"What a team!" said Mayor Goodway.

"If you ever need some All-Stars, just yelp for help!" said Ryder.

Ryder smiled at the pups. "You've all been very good pups – and players!"